Now I am a Fairy

Now I am a Fairy

Annabel Morgan

photography by Katy McDonnell

illustrations by Hannah Watchorn

styling by Rose Hammick

RYLAND
PETERS
& SMALL

LONDON NEW YORK

Designers **Pamela Daniels & Carl Hodson**
Commissioning editor **Annabel Morgan**
Picture research **Emily Westlake**
Production **Gemma Moules**
Publishing director **Alison Starling**

Fairy Cooking recipes adapted from
recipes by **Caroline Marson**.

First published in the United States
in 2007 by Ryland Peters & Small, Inc.
519 Broadway, 5th Floor
New York, NY 10012
www.rylandpeters.com

10 9 8 7 6 5 4 3 2 1

ISBN-10:1-84597-498-0
ISBN-13: 978-1-84597-498-5

Printed in China

Contents

This book belongs to

stick photo or
drawing here

A picture of me as a fairy

all about fairies

10

What fairies look like

Fairies are much smaller than humans. In fact, compared to us, they are tiny (about the size of your thumb, or a butterfly). They are almost invisible to the human eye, because they move so fast. But fairies can sometimes be spotted by the trail of fairy dust they leave hanging in the air behind them. Also, if you listen very carefully on a warm summer's evening, you may hear the echo of their tinkling laughter carried on the wind, or catch a glimpse of their gossamer-fine wings glinting in the last few rays of the sun.

Where they live

Fairies live mostly in trees and flowers, so forests and woods are full of them. At night, the fairies curl up inside the velvety petals of a rosebud, or under a soft green leaf. There might be fairies living at the bottom of your yard!

Fairies are great friends with small creatures and insects, such as ladybugs, butterflies, birds, bees, and squirrels. If you want to attract fairies to your yard, remember that they love pretty, shiny things. So you could hang wind chimes or sparkling mirrors from a tree. Fairies are great friends with the birds, so a birdhouse or a bird-feeding station will draw many birds, who will in turn bring their fairy friends with them.

11

What fairies do

Fairies are playful, friendly little creatures. They spend their days laughing, singing fairy songs, practicing their magic, and casting spells. Young fairies go to fairy school, where they learn to use their wands properly, to fly swiftly and gracefully, and to cast spells.

Fairies make kind and loving friends, and have excellent manners, but they often have a naughty streak. Fairies can be rather mischievous, and enjoy playing tricks on humans and each other!

What they eat

Fairies eat fairy food—fruit, nectar from flowers, or honey brought to them by friendly bees. They drink dewdrops from tiny acorn cups. Fairies also have a very sweet tooth, and on special occasions they love holding fairy tea parties, with yummy cupcakes to nibble on. Turn to page 40 to find some recipes for extra-specially delicious fairy food!

Making a magic wand

1) **Cut out.** To create a template for the wand, use two star-shaped cookie cutters, one bigger and one smaller. On a piece of paper, draw around them both so you have a star within a star, as shown. Cut out the template and use it to cut two star shapes from stiff card. If you only have white card, you can paint the stars any color you want.

2) **Paint.** Paint the wood dowel rod and the metal bell white. You may have to apply several coats for an even finish. Seal with a coat of clear water-based varnish, if desired.

3) **Assemble.** Thread all the bells onto short pieces of silver thread. Place one star face down. Arrange a jingle bell at each point and the larger bell in the center, as shown. Apply glue to the wrong side of the second star and stick it firmly on top of the first one, making sure the bits of thread and the end of the dowel rod are sandwiched between the stars.

4

4) Decorate. Cut four 4in (10cm) lengths of craft wire, and thread a charm onto each one. Twist the end of the wire over to hold the charms in place. Wind the ends of the wire round the wand just beneath the star. Now tie the ribbons round the wand so they conceal the wire. Allow the ribbons to hang down loosely. Now you can wave your wand and cast magic spells!

15

fairies and their other
magic friends

18

Pixies

Pixies are tiny, willful little folk with pointy ears. In the olden days, some people would leave out dishes of food or milk for the pixies to eat at night-time. They believed that the pixies would be so grateful that they would tidy up the house and not play any mischievous tricks!

Gnomes

Gnomes cannot fly and live underground. They like the dark and often make their homes under oak trees. Gnomes wear pointy hats and have long white beards.

Imps

Like pixies, imps love playing tricks on each other as well as on human beings! They are often held responsible for missing or moved articles (such as socks or keys) and for causing minor accidents like stubbed toes. Ouch!

19

Leprechauns

Leprechauns are from Ireland. They are said to be greedy and cunning characters who dress all in green from head to toe. Leprechauns are fairy cobblers or shoemakers, and make shoes for the elves. Leprechauns are often very rich. They love collecting gold and anything gold-colored. It's said that they hide their golden treasure in pots at the end of the rainbow!

Sprites

Tiny, lively sprites are the smallest of all the fairies. They love water and often live by quiet, tranquil ponds and creeks, alongside their friends the dragonflies.

Goblins

Goblins are small and hairy with big ears and look like little old men. They are very shortsighted, with husky, high-pitched voices, and often have long beards and pointy noses. Like gnomes, goblins live underground, deep in a magic kingdom ruled over by the king of the goblins. Traditionally, goblins are the sworn enemies of the elves.

Elves

Elves are often mentioned in old folk tales and songs. They are easily identified by their long, pointed ears and are generally believed to be small, shy people with playful personalities. Unlike many kinds of fairies, elves do not have wings. As most people know, elves help Santa Claus to make toys and wrap Christmas presents in his workshop at the North Pole!

21

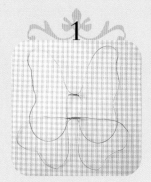

1) Form the framework. Gently bend the craft wire into the shape of butterfly wings. Pinch the wings together in the center to form the shape shown (the top pair in the picture, left) and fix in place with the tape. Now make the lower pair of wings, imitating the shape shown in the picture and again taping them together in the middle.

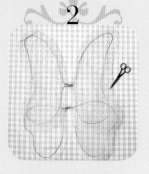

2) Glue on the net. Using the wire wings as a template, cut wing shapes from the piece of net, making sure you leave an extra 2in (5cm) margin all the way round. Place the net wing shapes face down on a table. Apply a thin line of glue to the wire frame, then firmly place it on top of the matching fabric shape. Repeat with the second set of wings. Leave to dry.

3) Attach the wings and elastic. When the glue is dry, use scissors to snip all around the edges of the net to create a fringed effect. Cut a piece of elastic 3ft (1m) in length and knot the ends to form a loop. Fold the loop in half and hold it in the middle. Put the wings together and place the center of the elastic over the center point of the wings. Fix the wings and elastic together using duct tape.

Making fairy wings

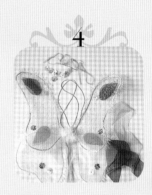

4) Decorate the wings. Cut leaf shapes from the gauze ribbon and glue them and the sequin flowers to the wings. Conceal the wire framework of the wings by glueing a narrow ribbon in place over it. Finally, cut three or four pieces of satin ribbon 16in (40cm) in length. Fold them in half and attach them to the center of the wings by winding a piece of feather trim round the ribbons to secure them. To wear the wings, slip your arms through the elastic loops.

23

The tooth fairy

When a child loses one of his or her baby or milk teeth, they leave it under their pillow at bedtime. It's the tooth fairy's job to collect the tooth and replace it with a lovely shiny gold or silver coin. Some people believe that the tooth fairy takes all the little baby teeth up to the dark blue night sky, where they are turned into the twinkling stars you can sometimes see from your bedroom window!

The Sugar-plum fairy

The story of the Sugar-plum fairy comes from a famous ballet called *The Nutcracker*. A little girl named Clara receives a new nutcracker for a Christmas present. After lots of exciting adventures, the nutcracker turns into a handsome prince and takes Clara to visit the Land of Sweets, where they are greeted by the beautiful Sugar-plum fairy, who dances specially for Clara and the prince.

Fairy godmother

Many fairy tales have a fairy godmother, but the most famous one is in the story of *Cinderella*. When Cinderella's cruel stepmother and stepsisters go to a ball at the royal palace, leaving Cinderella crying alone at home, her fairy godmother appears and uses her magic powers to change a pumpkin into a coach, six mice into fine white horses, and Cinderella's rags into a ballgown.

With the help of her fairy godmother, Cinderella goes to the ball and the handsome prince falls in love with her! However, the fairy godmother's magic only lasts until midnight. Even though Cinderella runs away when the clock strikes midnight, the prince manages to track her down by making every girl in the kingdom try on the glass slipper that Cinderella dropped as she left the ball. They have a beautiful wedding and Cinderella's fairy godmother is a very special guest!

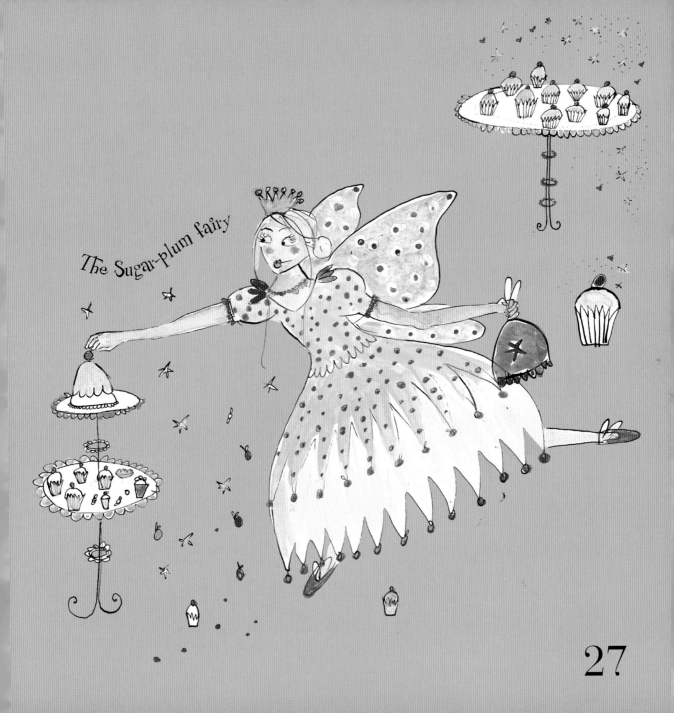

The Sugar-plum fairy

27

The bad fairy

The story of *Sleeping Beauty* tells of a king and queen who had a baby daughter. They invited all the fairies in the kingdom to a party to celebrate. Each fairy gave the baby a special gift. Just as the last fairy was about to give her gift, a bad fairy entered. She was very angry that the king and queen had not invited her to the party! She placed the baby princess under a spell, saying that at the age of fifteen she would prick her finger on a spinning wheel and die. The last good fairy could not undo the spell, but she changed it, saying the princess would not die, but would fall into a long sleep until awoken by a kiss from a prince.

Sure enough, on her fifteenth birthday, the princess pricked her finger on a spinning wheel and she (and everyone else in the castle) fell into an enchanted sleep. Many years later a handsome prince fought his way through the forest of thorns that had grown up around the castle and woke Sleeping Beauty with a kiss. The prince and Sleeping Beauty were married and lived happily ever after!

Tinkerbell

In the story of *Peter Pan*, Tinkerbell is Peter's guardian fairy. She has a sparkling wand and when she sprinkles fairy dust, it gives people the power to fly. Tinkerbell is very jealous of Peter's new friend Wendy, who he brings to Neverland to look after his friends the Lost Boys. She plays some mean tricks on Wendy, which makes Peter very cross!

Titania, queen of the fairies

Hundreds of years ago, a very famous writer called William Shakespeare wrote a play entitled *A Midsummers Night's Dream*. It tells the story of the adventures of the beautiful Titania, the queen of the fairies, and her husband, Oberon, who is the king of the fairies. Titania has four little fairy helpers named Peaseblossom, Cobweb, Moth, and Mustardseed.

You will need:
a pair of ballet slippers (be old or new), 2yds (2m) satin ribbon, scissors, clear glue, tiny jewel shapes, stick-on flower decorations, net fabric in two colors, a needle and thread, leaf-shaped sequins.

Making fairy shoes

1

1) Decorate the slippers and ribbon. Cut four equal lengths of satin ribbon, two for each slipper. Using clear glue, attach a line of tiny jewels to each length of satin ribbon. Leave to dry. Now glue the flower decorations to the ballet slippers in a pretty design and leave to dry completely.

2

2) Cut out the leaf shapes. Cut small leaf shapes from the two different-colored net fabrics. Sew them all the way around the top edge of each ballet slipper, alternating the two colors. Now attach two ribbon ties to each slipper. Stitch them firmly to the inside of the slippers at either side of the heel.

30

3

3) The finishing touches. Finally, attach the leaf-shaped sequins to your ballet slippers. Place them at regularly spaced intervals on top of the net leaves, and stitch them firmly in place.

31

Making fairy dust

It's easy to make pretty fairy dust from left-over pieces of colored scrap paper or gift wrap. You will also need some craft paper punches in three or four different designs. We used flower, heart, and butterfly punches to make the fairy dust shown here. Keep the fairy dust in a little bag and scatter it around when you cast a magic spell.

Magic wand practice

To practice using your magic wand, stand in a large space (outside in your yard is a good place) and hold your wand firmly. First, point it straight in front of you and move it in circles that start off very small then slowly get bigger and bigger (this is how fairies wave their wands when they are casting a spell).

Now slowly turn in a circle, using just your wrist to wave your wand gently up and down (this is the way fairies scatter fairy dust from the end of their wands). Finally, practice waving your wand in a quick, snapping motion. This is how fairies wave their wands when they want to make things disappear!

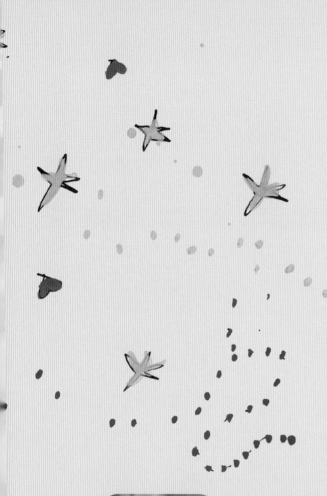

35

Fairy spells

Why don't you create a special fairy spell book from a scrapbook or an exercise book? First of all, cover the outside of the book with some pretty gift wrap (a grown-up could help you with this) or, if you prefer, some plain white paper that you can draw pictures of fairies on. Now have fun decorating your spell book with glitter glue, stickers, cut-out pictures from magazines, and any other sparkly bits and pieces that you can find. Use metallic pens or markers to write SPELL BOOK on the front in your best handwriting.

A spell for good luck

Ingredients:
★ A handful of uncooked white rice
★ Ten tiny pebbles
★ A handful of dirt
★ An acorn
★ A feather
★ A bright green leaf

Using a small forked twig, mix all the spell ingredients in a glass jelly jar. In the yard, dig a little hole. Unscrew the jar and pour the contents into the hole, whispering the following words:

Shooting stars and magic wands
Wishing wells and fairy dust
Fairies big and fairies small
Bring me magic fairy luck!

Carefully cover the spell ingredients with fresh dirt then tap the area three times with your wand.

A spell to stay best friends forever and ever (make this with your best fairy friend)

Ingredients:
* ★ The petals of four roses, two roses plucked by you and the other two by your best friend
* ★ 8 tablespoons of rainwater (collect rainwater in a plastic water bottle that your mom has cut in half. Put it outside on a balcony or in the garden so it can collect rain)
* ★ A handful of grass cut with a pair of silver-colored scissors
* ★ A handful of daisy heads

Mix all the ingredients together in a glass jar. Screw on the lid and take turns to shake it well. Place the jar on the ground in a circle of green leaves that you have picked together. Both fairies must take their wands in their hands and tap the jar on the lid three times, saying "fairy friends never end" each time.

Making a fairy crown

1

1) Assemble the crown. For the crown, we used a fabric headband from an accessories store. Take your leaves then, using pieces of fine-gauge craft wire 8in (20cm long), thread a wire through the spine of each leaf then bring the two ends together and twist. Wrap the other end of the wire tightly round the headband.

2

2) Add the decorations. Now you can start to glue your chosen decorations to the leaves. We used sequin flowers to add a touch of sparkle. We also used a few lengths of silver wire to create tendrils. Wind one end of the wire around a pencil several times then slide it off and wrap the other end round the headband.

3

3) The finishing touches. Continue to add stars and flowers until you are happy with the effect. Now attach the feather butterflies by twisting the end of the wire around the headband. Finally, take a length of ribbon and wind it all the way around the headband so all the wire is concealed. Finish with a dot of strong glue to hold the ribbon in place, and leave to dry thoroughly before wearing your fairy crown!

39

fairy
cooking

Fairy cupcakes

Little fairies will enjoy munching on these cupcakes, which have an unusual and delicious cream-cheese frosting.

Ingredients:

1 tablespoon milk
3 eggs, lightly beaten
½ cup (100g) superfine sugar
generous ¾ cup (115g) self-rising
   flour
¾ stick (85g) butter, melted

cream-cheese frosting:
⅔ cup (150g) low-fat cream
   cheese
¾ cup (100g) confectioners' icing
   sugar
zest of 1 unwaxed lemon or
   orange, plus 2 tablespoons
   of juice
cake sprinkles and candy shots,
   for decorating

Makes 15 cakes

Method:

1. Preheat the oven to 375°F (190°C). Line a muffin tray with 15 paper muffin cups.
2. Using an electric beater, beat the milk, eggs, and sugar in a bowl until thick and glossy and doubled in bulk (it should leave a trail when the beater is lifted). Add half the flour and half the butter and fold until evenly distributed, then fold in the remaining flour and butter.
3. Using a tablespoon, fill the muffin cups almost to the top. Bake for 10 minutes until risen and golden. Cool on a wire rack.
4. For the frosting, beat together the cream cheese, confectioners' sugar, and zest and juice of the orange or lemon until smooth.
5. When the cakes are cool, slice a small circle off the top of the cakes, then cut it in half. Fill the hole with a little frosting and push the two halves into the icing to form a butterfly shape. Decorate with sprinkles and candy shots.

Delicious!

Magic fruity smoothies

These yummy fruity drinks are healthy and delicious.

Makes 4 smoothies

Ingredients:

2 x 8oz pots (1 x 420g pot) of
   vanilla yogurt
1 banana
a handful of strawberries, hulled
any other fruit you have at home
2 tablespoons honey

Method:

1. Whizz all the ingredients together in a blender.
2. Pour into tall glasses and serve.

Yum yum...

Fruit kebob "magic wands"

Ingredients:

16 strawberries, hulled
24 seedless green grapes
4 kiwi fruit, peeled and sliced
24 blueberries

Method:

Thread the fruit onto 8 wooden skewers. Serve with yogurt or warm chocolate sauce.

Makes 8 kebobs

Fairy krispies

These are easy and fun to make and look so pretty—perfect for a fairy tea party!

Ingredients:
⅛ stick (15g) butter
1 tablespoon runny honey
1 tablespoon demerara sugar
2 cups crisped rice cereal
¾ cup (40g) mini marshmallows
pastel-coloured sprinkles

Method:
1. Preheat the oven to 350°F (180°C). Line a muffin tray with 18 muffin cups.
2. Put the butter, honey, and sugar in a small pan and stir over the heat until the butter has melted.
3. Add the cereal and mix well. When the mixture has cooled slightly, add half the marshmallows and mix again. Divide the mixture between the muffin cups.
4. Bake for 8–10 minutes or until lightly browned. Remove from the oven, and allow to cool.
5. Decorate with the remaining marshmallows and sprinkles.

Scrumptious!

Makes 18 yummy krispies

Having a fairy tea party

Now you've read all about fairies, why don't you have a special tea party for your very best fairy friends? Here you can make a list of the guests and what you're going to give them to eat.

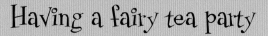

Fairy tea party guest list

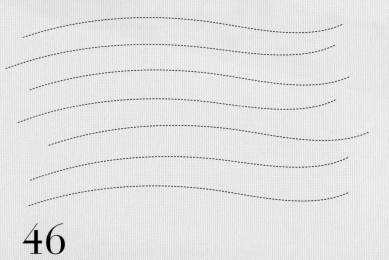

Fairy menu

46

This is to certify that

----

has now officially become
a fairy of the highest order

Picture credits and sources

Picture credits

Maggie Bulman Costumes
020 9693 9733
www.enchantedcastle.co.uk
*Pages 2 & 37: daisy flower fairy
costume; Page 29: wings; Page
39: butterfly fairy top.*

Grace and Favour
35 North Cross Road
London SW11 9ET
020 8693 4400
*Page 25: cushion, bedding, little
beaded pot.*

North Cross Road Market
London SE22
(Fridays & Saturdays only)
*Page 13: children's tea set,
hanging butterflies; Page 41: tea
set, cake stands, peg dolls,
hanging decorations, sparkly
butterflies.*

All make-up and hair by Hazel
Burford (hjburford@hotmail.com)

General sources

The Baker's Kitchen
3326 Glanzman Rd.
Toledo, Ohio 43614
419-381-9693
www.thebakerskitchen.com
*Cake decorating, candy making,
baking and kitchen supplies.*

**The Button Emporium &
Ribbonry**
914 S.W. 11th Avenue
Portland, OR 97205
503-228-6372
www.buttonemporium.com
Vintage and assorted ribbons

Candyland Crafts
201 W. Main Street
Somerville, NJ 08876
908-685-0410
www.candylandcrafts.com
*Baking and muffin cups, cookie
cutters, and cake decorations.*

Discount Dance Supply
www.discountdance.com
Ballet slippers.

JoAnn Fabrics
Locations nationwide
Visit www.joann.com for details of
your nearest store.
Art and crafts supplier

Just Kid Costumes
1-888-821-4890
www.justkidcostumes.com
Fairy costumes.

Pottery Barn Kids
www.potterybarnkids.com
*Cute bedding, tableware, and
dress-up costumes for little fairies.*

Willow Tree Toys
877-800-TOYS
www.willowtreetoys.com
*Fairy costumes, slippers and
magic wands.*

Thank you to our special
fairy models: Abigail,
Aisha, and Ruby!